Rock 'n' Roll

2nd Grade

Rock 'n' Roll

by ABBY KLEIN

illustrated by JOHN McKINLEY

Scholastic Inc.

To Teddy,
Welcome to the family!
XOXOXO
Lots of love,
A.K.

ISBN 978-0-545-93178-6

10 9 8 7 6 5 4 3   19 20 21

Printed in the U.S.A.   40

First printing 2017

Book design by Mary Claire Cruz

CHAPTERS

I have a problem. A really, really big problem. My favorite band, the Beat Boys, is having a contest. You have to make a music video of their newest song. If they like your video the best, then you win free tickets to their next concert, and you get to meet the band! I really want to win, but I'm not a very good dancer.

Let me tell you about it.

CHAPTER 1

Boppin' to Breakfast

"Freddy!" my mom called from downstairs. "Where are you?"

I didn't answer. I was too busy watching a video on my mom's phone.

"Freddy!" she called again. "Get down here right now! You're going to be late for school."

I still didn't answer.

"Freddy! I know you can hear your mother," said my dad. "Do I have to come up there and get you? Because if I do, there will be a consequence!"

A consequence. I didn't want that. "No! No!

I'm coming!" I yelled back. "Be there in a minute!"

I bounded down the stairs with the phone in my hand and bebopped into the kitchen.

"Ha! Ha! Ha!" said my sister, Suzie, pointing and laughing at me.

I ignored her.

"Ha! Ha! Ha! That is the funniest thing I've ever seen," she continued.

"Freddy," said my mom. "What are you doing with my phone?"

I just stared at the screen.

"Freddy, give me that phone," she said, and yanked it out of my hand.

"Awwww. I was just getting to the best part."

"Well, you're so busy watching that video that I think you forgot something."

"You forgot something, all right," Suzie said, and burst out laughing again.

"What is your problem?" I said to Suzie. "You are so annoying."

"Are you planning on going to school today?" asked Suzie.

"Of course I'm planning on going to school," I answered. "That's a stupid question."

"Really?" said Suzie, snickering.

"Yes, really."

"Like that?" said Suzie.

"Like what?"

"In your tightie whities shark underwear?"

I looked down at my legs. I didn't have any pants on! I guess I was so focused on the video that I forgot to put on my pants.

"Oops," I said, blushing.

"I think you need to run back upstairs and put some pants on," said my dad.

"Yeah, that would probably be a good idea," I said.

"Or you could go like that," said Suzie. "I would love to see you get on the bus in your underwear."

"I'm sure you would," I said.

I ran out of the kitchen and raced up the stairs into my bedroom. I grabbed a pair of pants out of my drawer and threw them on. Then I bounded back down the stairs two at a time and skidded into the kitchen.

"Whoa! Slow down there," said my dad. "You're going to slip in your socks."

I sat down and picked up the phone that my mom had left on the table.

"What do you think you're doing?" said my mom.

"I just want to finish watching this video," I said.

"You don't have time for videos," s&. mom. "You have to eat your breakfast."

"I can watch and eat at the same time," I said, shoveling a spoonful of cereal into my mouth.

"Freddy," said my mom in her warning voice.

"Really, I can do both," I mumbled with a mouth full of cereal. Some milk sprayed out while I was talking.

"Eeeewwww! Eeeewwww!" Suzie cried, waving her hands in the air.

"What?" my dad asked.

"Freddy just spit milk in my face."

I swallowed what was in my mouth. "I did not."

"Yes, you did. I can feel it on my cheek. It's disgusting," said Suzie, wiping her face with a napkin.

"Freddy, how many times have I told you not to talk with your mouth full?" my mom asked.

"You are so gross when you eat," said Suzie. "You're like a pig."

"Suzie, that's not very nice to say," said my mom.

"Well, he is," said Suzie. "He's always got food coming out of his mouth."

"All right. Enough." My dad put down his coffee mug. "Freddy, give me that phone."

I looked at him. "But, Dad . . ."

"No buts," said my dad. "Give that to me now."

I handed him the phone.

"You know the rules. You're not allowed to bring this to meals."

"I know. I know," I said. "It's just that I wanted to see the new Beat Boys video, *Rock It*, before I got on the bus this morning because I know everyone will be talking about it."

"Did you just say the new Beat Boys video?" said Suzie.

"Yep."

"I didn't know it came out!"

"It just came out this morning," I said.

"No way!" said Suzie. "I had no idea. Can I watch it, Dad, please?"

"What did I just say? No watching videos at the breakfast table."

"But I'll be the only one who hasn't seen it. Can I just watch it for two minutes?" Suzie begged.

"No means no," said my dad. "You'll just have to watch it when you get home from school."

"I can't believe you got to see it, Freddy," said Suzie. "I totally forgot that it was coming out today."

"Well, you'd both better hurry up and finish your cereal," said my mom. "The bus will be here any minute."

I shoveled a few more spoonfuls of cereal into my mouth and washed it down with some orange juice.

"Is the video good?" asked Suzie.

"Good? It's better than good," I said. "It's awesome!"

"Really?" said Suzie.

I nodded. "I think it might be the best one yet!" I jumped out of my chair and did a few hip-hop moves.

"Freddy, stop dancing," said my mom. "Come over here for a minute. Your hair is a mess."

"I already brushed it."

"With what? Your fingers?"

"That is some of the worst bed head I've ever seen," my dad said, laughing.

I bounced over to my mom, and she tried to slick down a few unruly strands of hair with some water.

Just then the bus squealed to a stop outside our house.

"Well, that will have to do," said my mom. "You two had better run."

"Bye! See you after school," I called as I grabbed my backpack and bopped out the door.

CHAPTER 2

The Contest

I jumped on the bus and sang softly to myself as I made my way down the aisle to sit with my best friends, Robbie and Josh. "'Rock it. Yeah, yeah, I said rock it.'"

Max stuck his arm out into the aisle so I couldn't get past him. "What is that awful noise?" said Max. "It sounds like a sick cat."

I stopped singing and stared straight ahead. I didn't dare turn to look at the biggest bully in the whole second grade.

"Freddy was singing," said Jessie.

"Singing?" said Max. "You call that singing? Ha!"

"Yes, he was singing the new Beat Boys song, 'Rock It,' and I think it sounded pretty good," said Jessie.

I smiled at Jessie.

"Oh! Oh! I love that song!" said Chloe, jumping up out of her seat.

"No one asked you," said Max.

Chloe ignored Max and started singing

loudly, "'Rock it. Yeah, yeah, I said rock it all night.'"

"Hey, Max!" yelled the bus driver. "Move your arm so Freddy can go sit down. I'm waiting."

Max glared at me and dropped his arm. I quickly went to sit down next to my friends.

Chloe kept singing "'Rock it, rock it,'" at the top of her lungs. Then she spun around and pumped her fists in the air.

Max plugged his ears. "Make her stop!" he shouted.

"Chloe, I am also waiting for you," said the bus driver. "Everyone needs to be seated before I can start driving again."

"But I'm not done showing everyone my dance moves," said Chloe.

"You can finish at school," said the bus driver. "Right now I have other kids to pick up, and you're making us late."

Chloe stuck out her lower lip in a big pout and plopped down in her seat. "Sorry, guys. I'll have to show you the rest at school. I know the whole dance."

"No one cares," said Max. "You are such a show-off."

"No I'm not!" said Chloe.

"Yes you are!"

"No I'm not!"

Josh leaned over and whispered in my ear, "These two are unbelievable."

I nodded my head. "It's been like this since kindergarten."

"My mom says I am the best dancer," said Chloe.

"Of course she does," Robbie whispered.

"Your mom is crazy," said Max, making the cuckoo sign by the side of his head.

"No she's not!" Chloe whined, stamping her foot.

"Cuckoo. Cuckoo," Max repeated.

"You don't know what you're talking about," said Chloe. "She says I am such a good dancer that I am going to win the Beat Boys contest."

Max got silent and stared at Chloe.

"Uh-oh!" I said to my friends. "What is he about to do?" I held my breath.

To my surprise, Max didn't do anything. He just asked, "Did you just say, 'Beat Boys contest'?"

Chloe nodded. "Yes, I did."

"What Beat Boys contest?" said Max.

"Are you kidding me?" I said to Josh and Robbie. "Everyone knows about the contest."

"The Beat Boys contest that I'm going to win," Chloe said, smiling and pointing to herself.

"What contest?" Max shouted.

"Max, please keep your voice down," said the bus driver. "No yelling on the bus."

"What contest?" Max repeated.

"The Beat Boys are having a music video contest," said Jessie. "You have to make your own music video of their new song, 'Rock It,' and if they think it's the best one, then you get free tickets to their next concert, and you get to meet the band."

Max's mouth dropped open. "No way!" he said.

"Yes way!" Chloe squealed. "And I'm going to win! I'm the best dancer out of everyone!"

"Stop bragging so much," said Jessie. "No one likes a bragger."

"I'm not bragging. I'm just telling you what my mom said."

"Of course she's going to say that," said Jessie. "Parents always tell their kids that they're the

best. My mom always tells me that I am the best soccer player, but that doesn't mean that I am."

I leaned over and whispered to Jessie, "You really are the best soccer player."

Jessie smiled. "Thanks, Freddy."

"Besides," said Max, "do you know how many kids are going to enter that contest? Like, a million!"

"It is a really cool contest," said Josh. "I think the three of us should enter."

"You're crazy," I said.

"Yeah," said Robbie. "Really crazy."

"Why?" asked Josh.

"Didn't you just hear what Max said? Everyone on the planet is going to want to enter this contest."

"So? We have as good a chance as anyone."

"No, we don't," said Robbie.

"Why not?" said Josh.

"Because you have to sing," I said.

"And dance," said Robbie.

"You just heard Max say I sounded like a sick cat."

"Why do you pay attention to anything he says?" said Josh. "He's always saying nasty things just to be mean. Besides, you don't have to really sing. You just have to lip-synch."

"Still, I can't dance."

"Robbie can dance," said Josh. "I've heard he's really good at hip-hop."

"Well, I don't know if I'd say I was *really* good," said Robbie.

"We can help each other," said Josh. "That's what friends are for!"

"I don't know," I said, hesitating.

"Come on, guys!" said Josh. "What do you have to lose?"

I shrugged my shoulders.

"Come on! Take a chance," said Josh. "You can't win if you don't even try."

"He does have a point," Robbie said.

I nodded. "But we'll have to practice a lot!"

"We can practice at recess and after school," said Josh. "We have a whole week to submit the video. That gives us a lot of time to practice."

Robbie turned to me. "I'll do it if you'll do it."

"All right! Let's do it!" I said.

We all high-fived each other as the bus pulled up at school.

We got off and started walking down to our classrooms.

"See you guys at recess for our first rehearsal!" Robbie called as he disappeared down the hall.

"We'll be there with our dancing shoes on!" Josh called after him.

CHAPTER 3

Recess Rehearsal

At recess, Josh and I waited for Robbie by our special meeting place. When he came out the door to the playground, we yelled, "Hey, Robbie, hurry up!"

Robbie came running up to join us by the big tree. "Sorry I'm late, guys. I was helping Miss Smith collect the math papers."

"That's okay," I said. "We just got out here, too, because we had to finish taking our spelling test."

"So let's start practicing our dance moves," said Josh.

"I'm going to need a lot of help with that!" I said, laughing.

"I'm sure you're not as bad as you think," said Josh.

"Just wait," said Robbie. "You may change your mind after you watch Freddy do a few moves."

"Hey, now, I'm not that bad, am I?"

Robbie laughed. "I'm just teasing you."

"Did you guys watch the video this morning?" asked Josh.

"YES! I think I watched it, like, three and a half times," I said.

"Three and a half?" Josh said, looking confused.

"I was in the middle of watching it for a fourth time when my mom took the phone away from me."

"Why did she take it away?"

"I accidentally spit cereal in Suzie's face," I said.

"How do you accidentally spit cereal in your sister's face?" said Josh.

"I bet I know how," said Robbie. "Freddy was probably talking with his mouth full. It's one of his bad habits."

"Yep. That's exactly what happened," I said.

"You need to learn to say it, not spray it," Josh said.

"Ha! 'Say it, don't spray it!' Suzie says that to

me all the time. I guess they say that in California, too!"

"Yeah, they do," said Josh, laughing. "So, Robbie, what about you? Did you watch the video?"

"Yes, but I only got to see it once because Kimberly was hogging our laptop."

"Boy, I'm glad I have a younger sister," said Josh. "Older sisters sound like a nightmare."

"Sometimes they're really great, but sometimes they can be a real pain," I said.

"You can say that again." Robbie laughed.

"Okay, guys, anyone have any ideas about how we should start?" asked Josh.

"Why don't you start like this," Chloe interrupted. "Just watch me."

"Where did she come from?" I whispered to Robbie.

"I don't know," Robbie whispered back. "It's like she popped up out of nowhere!"

Chloe started dancing and shaking her hips, her red curls bouncing around her head.

I covered my mouth with my hand so she wouldn't see me laughing.

"She really is cuckoo," said Robbie.

Josh stopped her. "Thanks, but I don't think we need your help."

"But I'm such a good dancer," said Chloe. "I know all the moves."

"Good, then you can make your own video," said Josh.

"Fine. You'll be sorry because mine will be way better than yours," Chloe bragged, and then she skipped away.

"I think she's from another planet," said Robbie.

We all laughed.

"Robbie, what do you think we should do first?" said Josh.

"Hmmm, let's see," said Robbie. "Let's try this. Step to the right, clap. Step to the left, clap. Step, step, jump, and clap."

"That doesn't seem too hard," said Josh. "What do you think, Freddy?"

"I think I can do that," I said.

"One, two, three, go," said Robbie. "Right, clap, left, clap . . ."

I started dancing and bumped into Robbie.

"Freddy, what are you doing?"

"Going to the right."

"You're supposed to go to the right *first* and then to the left. Watch me for a minute."

I watched Robbie carefully and counted the beat in my head.

"Do you think you're ready to try it again?" asked Robbie.

I nodded.

"Okay, let's try it again. One, two, three, go."

I took a step to the right and clapped, but then when I stepped to the left, I tripped over a tree root and fell down on my butt.

Josh started laughing. "Wow, Freddy, that was so graceful. Chloe should loan you one of her tutus."

"Ha-ha, very funny," I said. "I just tripped over this tree root."

"Here, let me help you up," Josh said, reaching out his hand.

I grabbed his hand, and he pulled me up.

"All right. One more time from the top," said Robbie. "One, two, three, go."

I stepped to the right and clapped. As soon as I turned to the left, I bumped right into Max.

"Hey, watch it, Sharkbreath," Max said.

"*You* watch it," I mumbled.

Max turned around, grabbed my shirt,

and pulled my face close to his. "What did you say?"

I gulped. "Nothing," I whispered.

"I know you said something," said Max, tightening his grip on my shirt. "What did you say?"

I gulped again and tried to look away.

"Let go of him," said Josh.

"Why should I?" said Max.

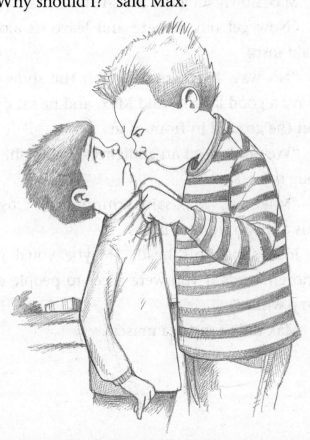

"Because I said so," Josh growled in Max's ear.

Boy, Josh was so brave. He was never afraid to stand up to the biggest bully in the whole second grade.

"Let go of Freddy right now," said Josh.

Max looked at me, and then he looked at Josh.

"Now!" Josh barked.

Max slowly let go of my shirt.

"Now get out of here and leave us alone," said Josh.

"No way, I'm here to watch the show and have a good laugh," said Max, and he sat down on the ground in front of us.

"We don't need an audience," said Josh. "Go bug someone else."

"Make me," Max said, grinning and crossing his arms in front of him.

Josh shook his head. "Maybe you'd have more friends if you were nicer to people once in a while."

Max didn't move a muscle.

"Come on, guys," said Josh. "We have to find another place to practice."

We started to walk away, but Max got up and followed us.

We walked over to the field, and Max followed. We walked over to the benches, and Max followed. We walked over to the basketball court, and Max followed.

Just then the bell rang for the end of recess.

"Oh well," said Robbie. "We'll just have to practice at Freddy's house today after school. At least no one can bother us there!"

CHAPTER 4

Rehearsal Part Two

I couldn't wait to get to my house after school so we could keep practicing for our video. The Beat Boys are my favorite band. I've always wanted to go to one of their concerts.

Robbie, Josh, and I burst through the front door and ran into the kitchen.

"Whoa, what's the rush, boys?" said my mom.

"We have a lot of practicing to do for our Beat Boys video," I said.

"*Your* video?" said my mom. "What are you talking about?"

"Remember how I was watching that video this morning on your phone at breakfast?"

"How could I forget?" my mom said, giggling. "You were dancing in your underwear!"

"Really?" Josh said, laughing. "You forgot to tell us that part, Freddy."

I blushed. "Thanks a lot," I mouthed to my mom. "Anyway, you know that's my favorite band, and right now they are running a contest. You have to make a music video of their new song, 'Rock It,' and if they pick your video you get free tickets to their next concert, and you get to meet the band!"

"That's pretty cool," said my mom.

"I know, right?" I said. "I just have to win that contest!"

"Well, you three had better get busy, but would you like a snack first?" asked my mom. "I just made some chocolate chip cookies."

"I will never say no to your chocolate chip cookies, Mrs. Thresher," said Robbie. "Yours are the best!"

"Thanks, Robbie," my mom said, smiling.

Josh took a bite of a cookie. "Wow! Robbie is right. These cookies are delicious."

We each grabbed a few more cookies and stuffed them into our mouths.

"Hey, Mom," I said. "Where are Suzie and Kimberly?"

"I think they went down to the basement," said my mom.

"Then we're going upstairs to my room," I said.

"All right, have fun."

We dashed up the stairs to my room. "Better close that door," I said to Josh. "We don't want Suzie and Kimberly snooping around and spying on us."

"Good idea," said Robbie. "Those two are so nosy."

"So now that we don't have Max and Chloe interrupting us," Josh said, "let's try doing the part Robbie was teaching us this morning at recess."

"Turn on the music, Freddy," said Robbie, "and I'll show you that part one more time."

I turned the music on really loud, and Robbie did the beginning steps while Josh and I watched.

"Do you think you have it, Freddy? I'm sure it will be easier for you to keep the beat now that you can hear the music."

"Yep. Let's try it," I said.

"All right, one, two, three, go," said Robbie.

I stepped right and clapped, then left and clapped, step, jump, clap.

"That was better," said Robbie.

"Yeah, at least you didn't bump into anyone this time," Josh said, chuckling.

"But after you go to the left," said Robbie, "you have to step twice before you jump and clap. You only took one step before you jumped. It goes step, step, then jump, clap."

"Oh, right. I forgot," I said. "Let's try it again."

We turned up the music and did it again.

"Yeah, dude, I think you got it that time," Josh said, giving me a high five.

We practiced it four more times. "Now you're getting the hang of it, Freddy," said Robbie. "See, you're not such a bad dancer."

I smiled. "You're a good teacher. What should we do for the next part?"

"I know!" said Josh. "Why don't we do the sprinkler?"

"The what?" said Robbie.

"The sprinkler. You know, like this," Josh said, putting one hand behind his head, extending the other arm straight out, and

flicking his hand back and forth while he moved the outstretched arm side to side.

"Where did you learn that?" I said.

"My dad taught it to me," said Josh.

"Your dad?"

"Yeah, he's always doing goofy stuff like that."

"Your dad sounds cool," I said.

"I think it's kind of funny," said Robbie. "If we put it in the video, maybe the Beat Boys will also think it's cool and start doing it, too!"

"Ha! That would be awesome!" said Josh. "I'll show you guys how to do it. Start the song over, Robbie."

Robbie turned the music back on, and we practiced doing the sprinkler.

When I turned the music down to work on the next part, I thought I heard a noise outside my door.

Robbie started to say, "So when—" but I put one hand over his mouth and a finger to my lips. Then I quietly pointed to the door.

Robbie and Josh turned to look in that direction. "What?" Josh mouthed.

I turned the music back up and then pulled the two of them closer to me and whispered, "I think I hear something outside the door."

"So?" whispered Josh.

"So I think it's Suzie and Kimberly spying on us."

"What should we do?" Robbie said.

"I have a plan," Josh whispered. "Let's pretend that we're practicing what we have so far, but I'll slowly tiptoe over to the door and yank it open. If they are leaning on the door listening, then they will fall into the room when I open it."

"That's a great idea!" I said.

"Shhh!" said Josh with a finger to his lips. "We don't want them to hear us. Are you guys ready?"

Robbie and I nodded.

"Should we try the whole thing one more time?" Robbie said loudly.

"Yeah, that's a good idea," I said.

"Get in your places," said Robbie. "All right. One, two, three, go!"

The three of us started to dance, and Robbie counted the beats out loud, "One, two, clap. One, two, clap," while Josh snuck over to the door.

"Good, Freddy, keep it up," said Robbie.

Now Josh was right by the door, with his hand on the doorknob. "Ready?" he mouthed to us.

We both gave him a thumbs-up.

Josh yanked the door open, and Suzie and Kimberly toppled into my room.

"Well, look who's here," I said as the girls scrambled to their feet.

"The two nosiest people on the planet," said Robbie.

Suzie and Kimberly turned to walk out, but Robbie and I grabbed them. "Not so fast," we said.

"What were you doing outside my door?"

"I'll tell you what they were doing," said Robbie. "Spying on us so they could steal some of our moves for their own video."

"Steal your moves? Ha! That's hilarious!" said Suzie. "Who would want to steal those moves? We just came up to have a good laugh."

"Well, you can get out of here now," I said. "And the next time we want a good laugh, we'll come spy on *your* rehearsal."

"Maybe you should," said Suzie. "You might actually learn something."

"Bye-bye," Robbie said, and we gently pushed them out the door.

"See ya!" I said, and slammed the door.

Josh shook his head. "Like I said, I'm glad I have a younger sister."

CHAPTER 5

Secret Spies

I waited a few seconds, and then I slowly opened my door to see if Suzie and Kimberly were still out there.

"Are they gone?" asked Robbie.

"Yep," I said. "Looks like they went back downstairs, but we'd better check in Suzie's room just to be sure."

"Good idea," Robbie said. "They could be hiding in there."

We tiptoed over to Suzie's room so they wouldn't hear us coming. Lucky for us, the door was wide open. I glanced around and then motioned for Josh and Robbie to follow me inside. Josh got down on his hands and knees and checked under the bed. Robbie opened the closet door and looked inside. I checked behind the bookshelf.

"I don't see them," said Robbie.

"Unless they know how to turn themselves invisible," said Josh. "I don't think they're here."

"Great! Come on, guys," I said. "Let's get back to our rehearsal."

"Hang on a minute," said Josh.

"Why?" I said.

"Look at these," Josh said, pointing to some rainbow clown wigs stuffed in Suzie's closet. "We should wear these in the video."

"No way!" said Robbie.

"Yes way," said Josh. "These are awesome! I love these!"

"The Beat Boys would definitely remember our video if we were wearing these," I said.

"That's true," said Robbie. "I didn't think of that."

"Come on! Try them on," Josh said, handing us each one.

We put them on, and all three of us burst out laughing. "HA! HA! HA! HA! HA!"

"What did I tell you?" said Josh. "These are perfect!"

"There's only one problem," I said.

"What's that?" said Josh.

"They belong to Suzie."

"So?"

"So she never lets me borrow anything that belongs to her," I said.

"Really?" said Josh.

I nodded. "Yep."

"So don't tell her you're borrowing them. You can just hide them in your room."

"But she'll see us wearing them in the video."

"So what? The video will already be made, so it will be too late for her to say no."

"I like that idea," said Robbie.

"Of course you do," I said, "because it's not *your* sister who's going to be mad."

"She'll get over it," said Robbie.

"Come on. Let's go back to Freddy's room and practice some more. I want to see what we look like dancing with these wigs on," said Josh.

We went back to my room and practiced our moves for about another half an hour. I had to admit, the wigs were pretty cool. They definitely added a special something.

"I'm dying to know what our sisters' routine looks like," said Robbie.

"Me, too," I said.

"They spied on us. So let's go spy on them," said Josh.

We all looked at each other and smiled.

"I like that idea," I said, "but we're going to have to be really quiet. I don't want my mom to see us, and I don't want the girls to hear us coming."

"We will have to be like secret ninja spies," said Robbie.

"Freddy, do you know where your mom is right now?"

"Let me check," I said. I tiptoed out of my room and listened at the top of the stairs.

I tiptoed back. "All clear," I said. "I can hear my mom talking on the phone in the den. She won't see or hear us walking down to the basement."

"Awesome!" said Josh.

"Let's go," said Robbie, "before she gets off the phone."

"You don't have to worry about that," I said, chuckling. "She can be on the phone for hours!"

We got to the top of the stairs, and I put my arm out to stop Robbie and Josh from going any farther.

"You have to skip the third step because it creaks," I whispered.

Robbie and Josh gave me a silent thumbs-up.

We tiptoed down the stairs, making sure we skipped the third step, and then we tiptoed through the living room and the kitchen to the top of the basement steps.

We could hear the music blaring. "We have to be extra quiet," I whispered. "We'll sneak down and then peek through the keyhole of the door. Okay?"

Robbie and Josh silently nodded.

We tiptoed down the stairs and hid behind the door. "I'll look first," I whispered.

I watched the girls do a few moves, and then I turned to Robbie and Josh. "They are really good," I whispered.

"Really?" said Robbie. "What are they doing that's so great?"

"See for yourself," I said, moving out of the way. Robbie crouched down to look. "Boy, you're not kidding, Freddy. They've got some cool moves."

"Cooler than ours?" said Josh. "Let me see."

Josh looked, then whistled softly. "Wow! You never told me your sisters could do backflips!" said Josh.

Josh must have whistled a little too loudly because before we knew what was happening, the door flew open, and we tumbled into the basement.

The girls were standing over us with their hands on their hips.

"I told you they were going to spy on us," said Kimberly. "I just knew it."

Suzie yanked the wig off my head. "Where did you get this?"

Oh no! We had forgotten to take the wigs off before our secret spy mission. I gulped. "It was . . . it was in my closet," I said.

"No, it wasn't," said Suzie. "These are mine. I had all three of them in *my* closet."

I just stared at her.

"You were snooping in my room. I'm going to tell Mom."

"No! Please don't," I said.

"What's it worth to you?" Suzie asked.

"Ummm . . . ummm," I stammered.

"I haven't got all day."

"I'll give you my dessert tonight," I said.

"Just tonight? I want your dessert for three nights, and then we have a deal," Suzie said, holding up her pinkie for a pinkie swear.

"How about two nights?" I said.

"It's three nights, or I tell Mom you were snooping in my room. Do we have a deal or not?"

"Fine, deal," I said as we locked our pinkies for a pinkie swear.

"Okay, you three clowns can get out of here now," said Suzie.

We raced up the basement stairs, dashed up to my room, and flopped on the bed.

"Wow!" said Josh. "Your sisters are good dancers."

Robbie and I nodded. "Really good," said Robbie.

"Too good," I said. "We'll never beat them."

CHAPTER 6

Teamwork

"So Mom told me the two of you are working on some videos for a Beat Boys contest," my dad said at dinner that night.

Suzie and I both started to talk at the same time.

"Hold on there," he said. "I can't hear you when you both talk at once. One at a time, please. Freddy, why don't you go first?"

"What?" said Suzie. "I started talking before he did. I should go first."

"Oh no you didn't!" I said. "I was talking, and you talked right over me like you always do."

"No I didn't!"

"Yes you did!"

"No I didn't!"

"Yes you did!"

"All right. That's enough, you two," said my dad. "If you don't stop arguing, then you'll both have to leave the table, and I won't hear the details from either one of you."

"Fine," I mumbled.

"Okay," Suzie muttered under her breath.

"Now, I have a compromise," said my dad. "You can take turns telling me all about it. Freddy, you can tell me one thing about the contest, and then Suzie can tell me something else about it. We'll keep going back and forth like that. Does that sound fair?"

We nodded our heads.

"Okay, so Freddy, your turn first."

"You know how I was watching that Beat Boys video this morning at breakfast?"

"Yes," said my dad.

"Well, that's their newest video. It's for a song called 'Rock It.'"

He turned to Suzie. "Your turn."

"So the Beat Boys are having a video contest. You have to make your own music video of that song 'Rock It.'"

"And if they think your video is the best, then you win free tickets to their next concert, and you get to meet the band!" I said.

"Kimberly and I are making a video because you know the Beat Boys are our favorite band," said Suzie. "I think I would die if I actually got to meet them!"

"And I'm making a video with Josh and Robbie. I've never been to a concert before. I really want to win!"

"That sounds like a really cool contest," said my dad. "I can understand why the two of you are so excited about it."

"Do you want to see some of the moves we have so far?" I said, jumping out of my seat.

I stepped to the right and clapped my hands, but when I went to step back to the left, I accidentally bumped into the table. My plate of spaghetti spilled onto the floor, and I slipped on the noodles.

"Oh my goodness! Freddy, are you all right?" my mom said, running over to me.

I looked up at her with a spaghetti noodle stuck to my cheek and another one dangling from my hair. "Yeah, I'm fine."

"We need to get this cleaned up right away," said my mom.

"If we had a dog, then you wouldn't have to clean this up," I said. "The dog would take care of it."

"Nice try," said my mom. "You know I don't like animals in the house." She was a neat freak. It was almost like she was allergic to messes.

I started to pick the noodles up with my hands.

"Freddy, no!" said my mom. "Not with your hands. First, come over to the sink so I can get the spaghetti out of your hair. Then I'll give you a sponge to clean that up."

I went over to the sink, and my mom pulled the noodles out of my hair and off my cheek.

"Now, take this," she said, handing me a sponge, "and go clean up that mess!"

It took me a while to get it all cleaned up, but eventually I sat back down at the table.

"No more demonstrations during dinner," said my dad. "If you want to show me something, then you can show me after dinner."

"Kimberly and I were working on our routine all afternoon," said Suzie. "I think it's pretty good."

"It's better than good," I said. "It's *really* good."

"How do you know, Freddy?" asked my mom.

"Yeah, tell Mom how you know," said Suzie.

"Well, we ummm . . . we ummmm . . ." I stammered.

"They spied on us," said Suzie, glaring at me.

"Only after they spied on us!" I shouted.

"You were spying on each other?" said my mom.

We both sat there silently.

"Your brother paid you a nice compliment," my dad said to Suzie. "He said your routine was really good."

Suzie turned to me. "Yours isn't bad, either," she said.

"Really?" I said.

"Really," said Suzie.

"But there's no way we can win without the

gymnastic stuff you and Kimberly can do," I said. "Those backflips are amazing."

"But your choreography is way better than ours," said Suzie.

"Robbie's really good at making up dance moves," I said. "You know he takes hip-hop classes."

"He does?" said my mom. "I didn't know that."

"Yeah, he goes to that dance studio by the mall."

"I have an idea," said my mom.

"What?" we both said together.

"Why don't the five of you make a video together?"

"What are you talking about?" said Suzie. "You think Kimberly and I should make a video with Freddy, Robbie, and Josh?"

"That's crazy," I said.

"Why?" my dad asked. "I think it's a good idea. Robbie can be the choreographer, and the girls can include some of their gymnastic moves."

"You'll have great dance moves and all of the cool flips and cartwheels," said my mom.

"It will be a winner for sure!" said my dad.

"I don't know . . . ," said Suzie.

I hesitated. "Me either," I said.

"Come on, work together," my dad said.

"You all will make a great team!" my mom said.

I looked at Suzie, and Suzie looked at me.

I shrugged my shoulders. "What do you think?"

Suzie shrugged her shoulders. "I guess it could work."

"Great!" my dad smiled. "And if you win, everyone will get to go to the concert."

"That's true," I said. "I never thought of that. I'm going to go talk to the guys."

"And I'm going to talk to Kimberly," said Suzie.

This might actually be a really great idea, I thought as I walked out of the kitchen. We just might win this contest after all.

CHAPTER 7

Sweet Moves

Suzie talked to Kimberly. I talked to Robbie and Josh, and we all decided to work together on the video. We practiced every day after school.

"I think the routine is looking pretty good," said Robbie.

"Pretty good?" said Josh. "I think we're looking more than pretty good. I think we're looking pretty *sweet*!"

"Sweet?" said Kimberly. "What's he talking about?"

I laughed. "That's one of Josh's California words that means awesome."

"I like that," said Kimberly. "I'll have to use that sometime."

"Remember, our dad has to shoot the video for us tomorrow," I said. "Then we have to upload it and enter it into the contest. The deadline is tomorrow at midnight."

"I'm so nervous," said Kimberly.

"Me, too," said Suzie.

"I just really want to win," said Robbie.

"I think we have a good chance," said Josh. "We have some super-cool moves that I bet no one else will have."

"You mean some *sweet* moves," Kimberly said, smiling.

Josh chuckled. "Yes, some super-sweet moves."

"Let's do the routine a few more times," said Kimberly. "Just so we make sure it's perfect before Freddy's dad shoots the video tomorrow."

"Good idea," said Robbie. "Everybody take your places. Start the music, Freddy. And one, two, three, go."

When we finished, Suzie said, "I think that was almost perfect."

"Almost," said Robbie, "but, Freddy, don't forget to freeze for that one beat right after the girls cartwheel over us."

"I know, I know," I said, hitting my forehead with the palm of my hand. "I have to count that in my head so I don't mess it up."

We all took our places one more time. I started the music over.

"And one, two, three, go!" said Robbie.

We started dancing, and I just kept thinking to myself, "Remember to freeze. Remember to freeze."

Right after the girls cartwheeled over us, I froze for that one beat. "Yes!" I whispered under my breath. "I did it!"

When the music stopped, we all high-fived each other.

"You did it, Freddy!" said Robbie. "You counted it perfectly."

Just then my mom knocked on the basement door.

"Anyone hungry?" my mom asked.

"Do you have more of those awesome chocolate chip cookies, Mrs. Thresher?" asked Josh.

My mom laughed. "Sorry, I don't have those, but I do have some warm brownies."

"Mmmmmmm, I thought I smelled

something delicious," I said, rubbing my tummy and licking my lips.

"You all have been working so hard that I thought you deserved a little reward," she said.

"Mom, before we go up to the kitchen to have our snack, do you want to see our routine?" said Suzie.

"I would love to," said my mom. "Your rehearsals have been top secret. I've been dying to see what you've been working on."

"Okay, get in your places everyone," said Kimberly.

"Freddy, start the music," said Robbie. "One, two, three, go."

When the music stopped, my mom started clapping wildly. "Oh my goodness! That was really amazing. I am so impressed. That was perfect!"

"Really?" I said, jumping up and down. "Do you really mean it, Mom? Is it really perfect?"

"I really mean it. I definitely think you all are ready to shoot your video tomorrow."

"Woo-hoo!" I shouted, and pumped my fist in the air.

"Now, how about a little treat?" she said. "Follow me."

We all went upstairs and stuffed our faces with brownies.

"These are delicious, Mom," I said as crumbs tumbled out of my mouth.

"Hey, say it, don't spray it," Josh said, flicking

a piece of brownie off his shirt. "I really don't want to wear your brownie."

Suzie laughed. "Freddy always talks with his mouth full. It's disgusting."

"Maybe I should wear my raincoat around you when you're eating in case it starts raining food," Josh joked.

I swallowed my last bite of brownie. "All done," I said.

"Is there anything else you all have to do before you shoot the video tomorrow?" asked my mom.

"We just need to finish getting our costumes together," said Suzie.

"What else are you guys wearing besides the clown wigs?" asked Kimberly.

"We're wearing neon T-shirts and gray sweatpants," said Josh.

"I'm wearing a lime-green shirt," said Robbie. "Josh is wearing a lemon-yellow shirt, and Freddy is wearing an electric-blue one."

"What about you guys?" I asked Suzie and Kimberly.

"Well, we need to look like a dance group," said Suzie, "so we should wear bright colors, too. We could wear our bright-pink leggings and purple tank tops."

"And we could wear our matching winter hats that are rainbow colors," said Kimberly. "The ones we got each other for Christmas."

"Great idea!" Suzie said. "They will match perfectly with the boys' wigs."

"No one can say our costumes are boring." Robbie laughed.

"That's for sure," Josh said.

"The Beat Boys will definitely remember us!" said Suzie.

"Okay, so everyone get your costumes together, and we'll meet back here tomorrow at three o'clock, so our dad can shoot the video," I said.

"I can't wait!" said Kimberly. "Come on, Robbie, let's go home and practice a few more times."

"Hey, I'll walk home with you guys," said Josh. "Bye, Mrs. Thresher. Thanks for the brownies."

"You're welcome," said my mom as she let our friends out the door. Then she turned to Suzie and me. "I am so proud of both of you."

"You are?" I said.

"Yes," she said. "Not only do you have a great routine, but you also worked well together. You were supportive and kind and helped each other just like teammates do."

"I'm actually glad you and Dad suggested Kimberly and I make a video with Freddy and his friends," said Suzie.

"Really?" I said. I couldn't believe my ears.

"Yes," said Suzie. "I've had a lot of fun, and you are actually a pretty good dancer, Freddy."

"I'm not that good. I'm just okay."

"You're better than okay," said Suzie. "Robbie choreographed some hard moves, and you can do them all. You shouldn't always be so hard on yourself."

"Thanks," I said, and smiled.

Sometimes older sisters can be really great.

CHAPTER 8

And the Winner Is . . .

The next day we made the video. We did it over and over and over. I think we made my dad shoot it about ten times because we wanted it to be perfect.

"Now we just have to upload it to the Beat Boys contest website," said Robbie.

"Do you need help with that?" asked my dad.

"No thanks, Mr. Thresher," said Robbie. "I can do it."

Robbie is a computer genius. He knows how to do almost anything on the computer.

We all huddled around Robbie while he posted our video.

"We have to give our group a name," said Robbie.

"How about Sweet Moves?" Kimberly suggested.

"Great idea!" we all said.

"Are you done yet?" asked Kimberly.

"Is our video entered in the contest?" asked Josh.

"Hold on, guys," said Robbie. "I'm almost done. It just takes a minute to upload."

Robbie pressed a few more buttons. "There," he said, smiling. "We have now officially entered the contest."

"Woo-hoo!" I yelled, and pumped my fist in the air.

"Do you think we'll win?" asked Suzie.

"Oh, I hope so," said Kimberly. "I really, really want to see the Beat Boys live in concert."

"Me, too," said Josh. "I've never been to a real concert before."

"Me neither," I said. "I've always wanted to go to one."

"Let's see if the website tells us how many people have entered the contest," said Robbie.

"Good idea," I said. "At least we'll know what our chances are."

"I bet a lot of people made videos," said Kimberly. "Everyone I know loves the Beat Boys."

"I'm guessing about five hundred people entered," said Josh.

"You're joking, right?" said Robbie. "It's way more than that!"

"Is it two thousand?" asked Kimberly.

"More!" said Robbie.

"More?" I groaned. "How many?"

"It looks like there are about five thousand videos posted right now, and people can still enter until midnight tonight!"

"We'll never win," I mumbled.

"Never say never. That's what my mom always says," said Josh.

"So what do we do now?" I said.

"We wait," said Robbie.

"We wait, and wait, and wait," said Kimberly.

"They aren't going to announce the winner for a week," said Robbie. "It says right here on the website that the winner will be announced next Friday at four o'clock."

"One week! I don't know if I'm going to be able to wait that long," I said. "I might explode from the excitement."

*   *   *

The whole week, it was really hard for me to think about anything else but the contest. I thought about it at night when I was in bed. I thought about it all day long at school. I even thought about it in the shower.

Friday finally rolled around. I bebopped down to breakfast and danced around the kitchen.

"Today's the day!" I shouted. "Today is the day we find out if we won the contest."

"Really?" my mom said, smiling. "I had no idea that today was the day. You've only been talking about it nonstop for the last week!"

I laughed. "I know. I know," I said. "I'm just really excited."

"Well, you have to go to school first," said my dad. "They aren't posting the winner until four o'clock."

"But I'm not going to be able to concentrate at school today," I said.

"Me neither," said Suzie.

"And I'm sure I'm going to have to listen to Chloe brag all day long about how she's the best dancer, and how she's going to win. Blah, blah, blah. She is so annoying."

"Just ignore her," said Suzie.

"It's hard to," I said. "She never shuts her mouth."

Suzie laughed. "That's true. She does talk a lot! She is such a motormouth."

"The bus will be coming any minute," said my mom. "Hurry up and grab your backpacks."

"Do we really have to go?" I whined. "Can't we just stay at home and stare at the computer all day? What if they post the winner before four o'clock?"

"Staring at the computer screen is not going to magically make the winner appear. They aren't going to post it early," said my dad.

"Besides," said my mom. "Going to school will make the time pass faster. Your mind will be on something else."

My mind will only be on one thing, I thought. *The contest, the contest, the contest!*

Just as I predicted, the day went by really slowly. I could not focus at all in class, and I had to listen to Chloe tell everyone over and over that she was going to be the winner because her nana told her so.

After school, Josh, Robbie, and Kimberly got off the bus at our house. We all ran into the

house, dropped our backpacks on the floor, and turned on the computer.

"Ooohh, I am so nervous," said Kimberly.

"I don't know if I can look," said Suzie, covering her eyes.

"My stomach is doing its own hip-hop dance right now," I said. "I think I'm going to throw up."

Josh laughed and took a step back. "Don't throw up on me, dude."

"I don't know how much longer I can wait," Suzie said.

"We've waited a week," said Robbie. "We can wait a few more minutes."

"It seems like time has stopped," Kimberly said.

We all stood there anxiously waiting for the winner to be posted.

"My heart is beating so fast I think it's going to explode!" I said. "I'm so excited. I might pee my pants."

Josh laughed.

"It's not funny," I said. "I really might have an accident."

"Cross your legs," said Josh.

Just then the clock on the computer switched to four o'clock.

"Here we go," said Robbie. "It will be posted any minute."

We all held our breath.

Then the name of the winner appeared on the screen.

I looked at it. Then I blinked and looked at it again. I couldn't believe my eyes! In big letters across the screen, it said, THE WINNER IS SWEET MOVES.

"AAAAAHHHHHH!" we all screamed. "We won! We won!"

"I can't believe it," said Josh.

"Me neither," said Kimberly. "I think I'm going to faint."

We all jumped around and high-fived and hugged each other.

"This is the best day ever!" I said.

"And I'm glad we all worked as a team, said Suzie, "because now we can all go to the concert together."

I hugged Suzie. "You're the best big sister in the whole world."

Suzie smiled. "You're not so bad yourself, little brother."

Freddy's Fun
Pages

START YOUR OWN BAND!

Want to have your own rock 'n' roll band? Try making these recycled instruments, and then grab some friends and rock out!

Guitar

You will need:

Pencil
Empty wrapping paper roll
Empty tissue box
Scissors
Rubber bands
Packing tape

Directions:

1. Trace the round end of your wrapping paper roll on each short end of the tissue box, then cut out the circles you traced. Make sure you trace your circles toward the back of the tissue box.

2. Thread your wrapping paper tube through the holes in your tissue box so about one inch sticks out of the bottom.

3. Cut off any plastic around the opening of your tissue box.

4. Reach inside the box and tape your wrapping paper tube to the back of the box with packing tape.

5. Stretch a few rubber bands lengthwise around the tissue box.

6. Pluck the rubber bands to make some sweet music!

Kazoo

Empty toilet paper tube
Wax paper
Rubber band
Markers
Scissors

Directions:

1. Decorate the tube with your markers.

2. Cut a six-inch circle from the wax paper.

3. Fit the wax paper circle over one end of your tube with a rubber band.

4. Make loud tooting sounds into the open end. Sound waves will vibrate the wax paper and make musical sounds!

Drum or Tambourine

You will need:

Two paper plates
Glue or staples
Markers
Plastic beads or dried beans

Directions:

1. Decorate the plates with your markers.

2. Staple or glue the plates together leaving a small opening at the top.

3. Drop a few handfuls of plastic beads or dried beans in between the plates.

4. Staple or glue the small opening closed.

5. Shake or tap on the plates to make music.

GET READY FOR FREDDY!

2nd Grade

READ THEM ALL!

Available in print and eBook editions

SCHOLASTIC